My First Pocket Guide

Illinois

By Carole Marsh

The GALLOPADE GANG

Carole Marsh
Bob Longmeyer
Michele Yother
Michael Marsh
Sherry Moss
Chad Beard
Sue Gentzke
Cecil Anderson
Steven Saint-Laurent
Deborah Sims
Andrew Brim
Andrea Detro
John Raines
Karin Petersen
Billie Walburn
Doug Boston
Kim Holst
Jennifer McGann
Ellen Miller
William Nesbitt, Jr.
Kathy Zimmer
Wanda Coats

Published by
GALLOPADE INTERNATIONAL

www.illinoisexperience.com
800-536-2GET • www.gallopade.com

Other Illinois Experience Products

- The Illinois Experience!
- The BIG Illinois Reproducible Activity Book
- The Incredible Illinois Coloring Book
- My First Book About Illinois!
- Illinois "Jography": A Fun Run Through Our State
- Illinois Jeopardy!: Answers and Questions About Our State
- The Illinois Experience! Sticker Pack
- The Illinois Experience! Poster/Map
- Discover Illinois CD-ROM
- Illinois "Geo" Bingo Game
- Illinois "Histo" Bingo Game

A Word From the Author... (okay, a few words)...

Hi!

Here's your own handy pocket guide about the great state of Illinois! It really will fit in a pocket–I tested it. And it really will be useful when you want to know a fact you forgot, to bone up for a test, or when your teacher says, "I wonder . . ." and you have the answer–instantly! Wow, I'm impressed!

Get smart, have fun!

Carole Marsh

Illinois Basics explores your state's symbols and their special meanings!

Illinois Geography digs up the what's where in your state!

Illinois History is like traveling through time to some of your state's great moments!

Illinois People introduces you to famous personalities and your next-door neighbors!

Illinois Places shows you where you might enjoy your next family vacation!

Illinois Nature - no preservatives here, just what Mother Nature gave to Illinois!

All the real fun stuff that we just HAD to save for its own section!

Who Named You?

Illinois' official state name is...

Illinois

Word Definition

OFFICIAL: appointed, authorized, or approved by a government or organization

Statehood: December 3, 1818

Illinois was the 21st state to join the United States.

Illinois' Native Name!

State Name Origin

Illinois is named for the Algonquin word *Illini* which means "men" or "tribe of superior men." It is taken from the word, *Illiniwek*, used to refer to the people who lived in the area. The Illini people were made up of many tribes who lived in what we call Illinois. They shared a similar language and customs. The French added *ois*, and that's how we get Illinois.

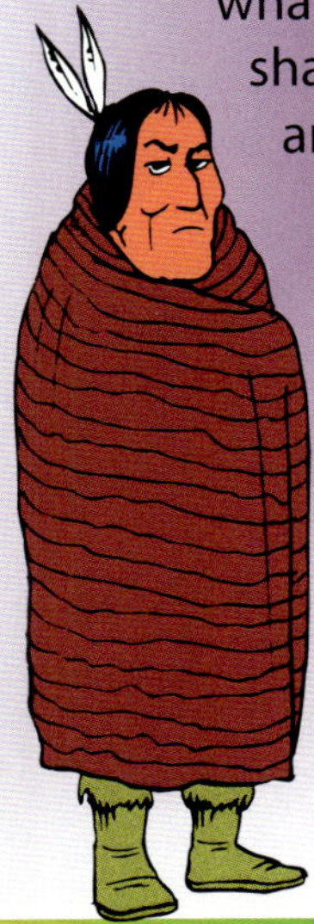

Names of Illinois places today reflect the early French influence; Joliet, Champaign, Dupage, Des Plaines, and La Salle are some examples.

What's In A Name?

Illinois is not the only name by which our state is recognized. Like many other states, Illinois has some nicknames, official or unofficial!

Prairie State

Land of Lincoln

Garden of the West

Crossroads of America

State Capital: Springfield

Established 1818

Since 1839

Kaskaskia was the state's first capital. In 1820, Vandalia became the temporary capital. Springfield, closer to the geographic center of the state, has been the capital since 1839.

The first settler on the site we now call Springfield was a farmer named Elisha Kelly. The city grew up around his home.

Word Definition

CAPITAL: a town or city that is the official seat of government

CAPITOL: the building in which the government officials meet

State Government

Who's in Charge Here?

Illinois' GOVERNMENT has three branches:

LEGISLATIVE | EXECUTIVE | JUDICIAL

The legislative branch is called the General Assembly.

- **LEGISLATIVE:** Two Houses: THE SENATE (59 members); HOUSE OF REPRESENTATIVES (118 members)
- **EXECUTIVE:** A governor, lieutenant governor, and other constitutional officers
- **JUDICIAL:** SUPREME COURT seven justices plus APPELLATE COURTS and CIRCUIT COURTS

To determine whether or not Illinois' state constitution is up to date, the general assembly is required to ask voters whether a constitutional convention should be called. This only happens every twenty years.

State Flag

The State Flag of Illinois was adopted in 1915. In 1970, a campaign began which led to the addition of the word *Illinois*. The flag is always found atop the state capitol, and all state, city, and town buildings.

State Seal

The Illinois state seal shows a shield which represents the original thirteen states, a bald eagle, and an olive branch.

Word Definition

MOTTO: a sentence, phrase, or word expressing the spirits or purpose of an organization or group

State Motto

State Sovereignty, National Union

The sunrise over the prairie on the state seal symbolizes the promise of a bright future.

Sovereignty means independent. Illinois is a state, but it also part of the United States of America.

Birds of Red Feathers

The state bird of Illinois is the Cardinal, *Cardinalis cardinalis,* known for its bright plumage and cheerful song.

The male cardinal has bright red feathers. Female cardinals have a red bill, but their feathers are a yellowish-brown.

White Oak

Illinois school students chose the oak tree as the state tree in 1907. In 1973, the white oak was specified as the state tree. The fruit of the white oak is called an acorn. White oaks are vulnerable to root rot caused by extreme weather and weed killers used on lawns. Gypsy moth larvae can kill a white oak by eating all of its leaves.

Violet

The violet became the state flower in 1907. In 1973, the native violet was specified in another vote by grade school students. There are over 400 species of violets throughout the world.

Violet flowers can be candied and are sometimes used to make jelly. The leaves can be added to salads.

Violet hybrids occur frequently in nature. Hybrid flowers are cross-pollinated. Insects can easily pollinate the flowers because of their open petals.

White-tailed Deer

In 1980, students voted the white-tailed deer Illinois' state animal. Males have antlers on their heads which are shed and regrown each year. The white-tailed deer raise their tail at approaching danger showing the white fur and warning following deer.

White-tailed deer are found throughout North America and the northern part of South America.

RIDDLE: If the state flower got mixed up with the state animal, what would you have?

ANSWER: A white-tailed violet... or a violet-tailed deer?

Tully Monster

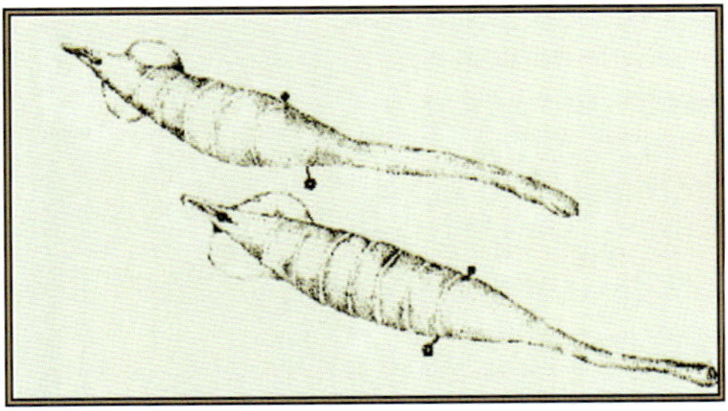

The Tully Monster, the state fossil, was a soft-bodied marine animal that lived 280 to 340 million years ago. More than 100 Tully Monsters have been found in Illinois. The Tully Monster became the Illinois state fossil in 1989. The creature was less than a foot long and probably not very scary. The monster was sort of like a tube, and did not have a backbone!

Fluorite

Fluorite, (sometimes called fluorspar) the state mineral, is combined with chemicals and used in the production of steel, aluminum, enamels, glass, and ceramics. Fluorite is found in different colors, and is sometimes brightly colored. The word fluorescent comes from fluorite.

☐ ***To Do List:*** Find out what your birthstone is. Can that gem be found in Illinois?

Fluorite is a glassy mineral which is found in veins in the ground as deep as 800 feet (244 meters).

Big Bluestem

Illinois' state grass is big bluestem. The grass is the tallest in Illinois. Sometimes the grass is called turkey-foot grass because it forks out at the top into three branches. It looks like a turkey's foot!

Illinois

Lyrics by C. H. Chamberlain
Music by Archibald Johnston

State Song

By the rivers gently flowing, Illinois, Illinois,
O'er thy prairies verdant growing, Illinois, Illinois,
Comes an echo on the breeze,
Rustling through the leafy trees, and its mellow
tones are these, Illinois, Illinois,
And its mellow tones are these, Illinois.

From a wilderness of prairies, Illinois, Illinois,
Straight thy way and never varies, Illinois, Illinois,
Till upon the inland sea,
Stands thy great commercial tree, turning all the
world to thee, Illinois, Illinois,
Turning all the world to thee, Illinois.

When you heard your country calling, Illinois, Illinois,
Where the shot and shell were falling, Illinois, Illinois,
When the Southern host withdrew,
Pitting Gray against the Blue, There were none more
brave than you, Illinois, Illinois,
There were none more brave than you, Illinois.

Not without thy wondrous story, Illinois, Illinois,
Can be writ the nation's glory, Illinois, Illinois,
On the record of thy years,
Abraham Lincoln's name appears, Grant and Logan,
and our tears, Illinois, Illinois,
Grant and Logan, and our tears, Illinois.

State Insect

The Monarch is found throughout the world but mainly in North America. Each fall, monarch butterflies migrate south to California, Florida, and Mexico. In its two-year lifetime, the monarch makes the trip twice.

Butterflies cannot fly if their body temperature is less than 86°F (30°C). At air temperatures below this, they must "warm up" their flight muscles by sunning their bodies or shivering their wings.

Bluegill

State Fish

The Bluegill is a member of the sunfish family. The Bluegill was made the state fish in 1986 in a vote by students. It is named for its colorful markings.

After the female bluegill lays its eggs, the male bluegill guards the nest.

Broiled Bluegill

Put a bluegill filet on foil. Drizzle with lemon juice. Sprinkle with salt and pepper. Add shredded smoked ham and broil fish until done.

The State of

Illinois

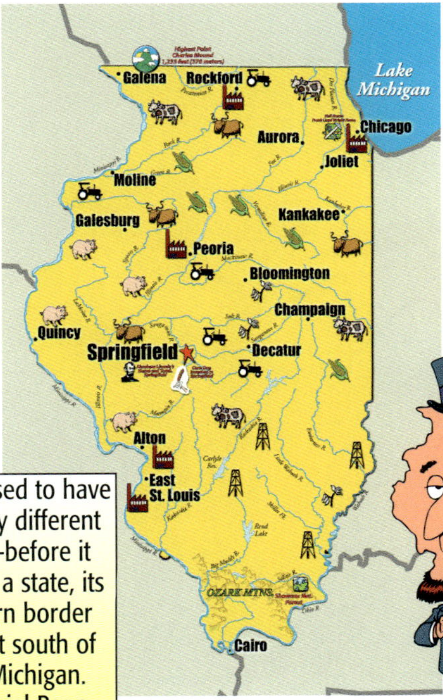

Illinois used to have a slightly different shape–before it became a state, its northern border was just south of Lake Michigan. Nathaniel Pope convinced the U.S. Congress to move the border 40 miles (64 kilometers) north giving Illinois access to shoreline on Lake Michigan.

Abraham Lincoln was part of a group of legislators who helped move the state capital from Vandalia to Springfield. You could say he helped "shape" the state.

State Location

Illinois is located in America's heartland. Its northern border touches the southern tip of Lake Michigan.

State Location

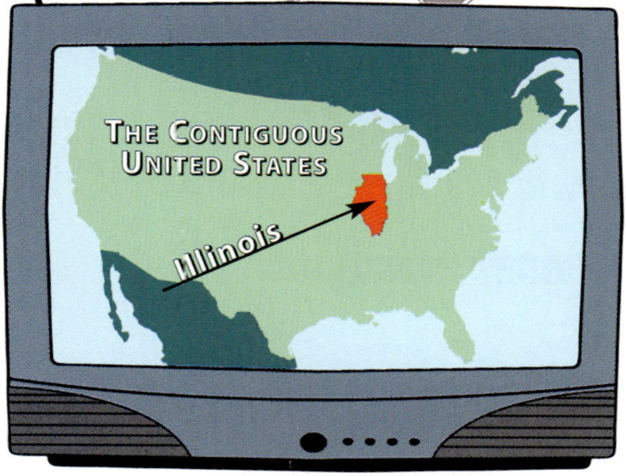

LATITUDE: Imaginary lines which run horizontally east and west around the globe
LONGITUDE: Imaginary lines which run vertically north and south around the globe

State Neighbors

On The Border!

These border Illinois:

States: Wisconsin, Kentucky, Iowa, Indiana, Missouri

Bodies of water: Lake Michigan, Ohio River, Wabash River, Mississippi River

I'll Take the Low Road...

Illinois is 213 miles (343 kilometers) east to west... or west to east. Either way, it's a long drive!

Total Area: Approx. 57,918 square miles
Land Area: Approx. 55,593 square miles

Illinois is 379 miles (610 km) north to south... or south to north. Either way, it's still a long drive!

You Take the High Road!

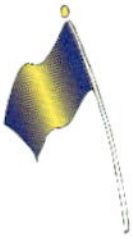

HIGHEST POINT

Charles Mound — 1,235 feet above sea level (376 meters)

Records indicate White Oak Fort was once located on Charles Mound. It was positioned here to help protect the Kellogg Trail, an old stagecoach road.

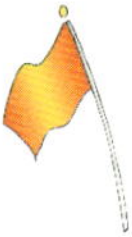

LOWEST POINT

On the Mississippi River in the extreme southwest — 279 feet (85 meters)

I'm County-ing on You!

Illinois is divided into 102 counties

Word Definition

COUNTY: an administrative subdivision of a state or territory

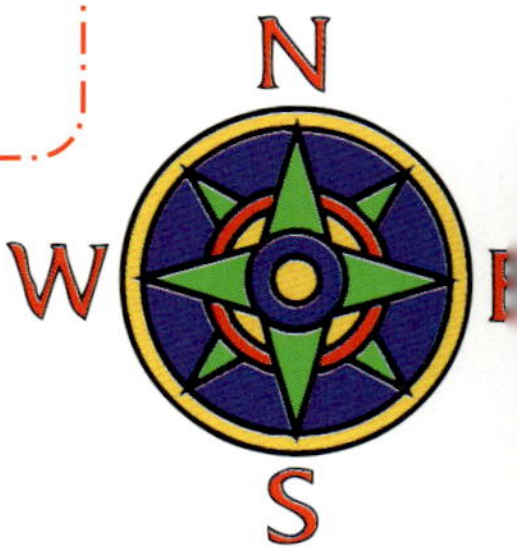

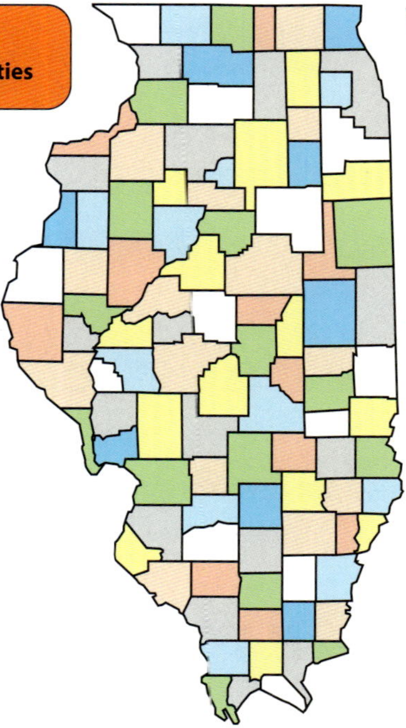

Natural Resources

Word Definition

NATURAL RESOURCES: things that exist in or are formed by nature

inerals:

- Coal
- Fluorite
- Tripoli
- Sand
- Petroleum
- Gravel
- Cement
- Lead

eep-water ports
ke Chicago and East St. Louis
low large ships to deliver and
xport goods around the world.

Weather, Or Not?!

Illinois gets every kind of weather including very hot and cold temperatures, thunderstorms, tornadoes, and blizzards. Cold air coming down from Canada, (called the Arctic Express!) can meet with warm air from the south causing storms and "lake effect" snow.

Highest temperature: 117°F (47°C), East St. Louis, July 14, 1954

°F=Degrees Fahrenheit °C=Degrees Celsi

Lowest temperature: -35°F (-37°C), Mount Carroll, January 22, 1930

In 1995, a severe heat wave in Illinois caused hundreds of deaths in Chicago. Summer temperatures often reach above 100°F (38°C).

Back On Top

Illinois' topography consists of wide open prairies and fertile plains throughout most of the state. There are some rolling hills in the southern region of the state and in the extreme northwestern portion of Illinois.

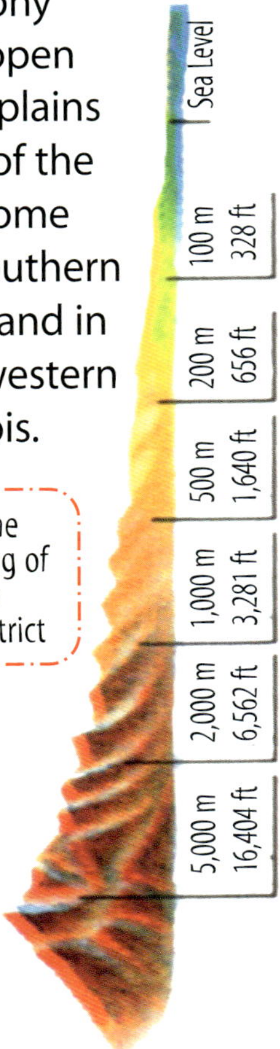

Topography

Word Definition

TOPOGRAPHY: the detailed mapping of the features of a small area or district

Illinois' fertile plains are ideal for farming. The state is second only to Iowa in the production of corn.

King of the Hill

Indian Mounds

The Cahokia Mounds and the Dickson Mounds give scientists a glimpse of early Native American life. Thousands of Indian mounds have been found in Illinois. Mounds were used for religious ceremonies and burials.

Shawnee Hills

The Shawnee Hills in southern Illinois are part of the foothills of the Ozark Mountains in neighboring Missouri. The Ozark-Shawnee Trail is a popular tourist trek, named for the Ozark mountains.

Down the River

The Illinois and Michigan canal linked Lake Michigan to the Mississippi River in 1848. Chicago became an important port city and a crossroad between two major waterways.

Here are some of Illinois' major rivers.

- Mississippi
- Wabash
- Ohio
- Saline
- Green
- Rock
- Spoon
- La Moine
- Kaskaskia
- Big Muddy
- Fox
- Des Plaines
- Kankakee
- Vermilion
- Salt
- Mackinaw
- Illinois
- Skillet Fork
- Sangamon

Gone Fishin'

- Lake Michigan
- Rend Lake
- Carlyle Lake
- Lake Shelbyville
- Orchard Lake
- Springer Lake
- Crystal Lake
- McCullom Lake
- Fox Lake

Many Illinoisans find relief from the heat at Chicago's public beaches on the Lake Michigan waterfront.

Word Definition

RESERVOIR: a body of water stored for public use

ARE YOU A CITY MOUSE... OR COUNTRY MOUSE?

Have you heard these wonderful Illinois city, town, and crossroad names? Perhaps you can start your own collection!

LARGER TOWNS:

Chicago
Rockford
Peoria
Springfield
Aurora
Naperville
Decatur
Arlington Heights
Elgin
Joliet

OTHER TOWNS:

Bone Gap
Sleepy Hollow
Monkey's Eyebrow
Coal City
Deer Creek
Red Bud
Walnut
Romeoville
Sunnyside
Energy
Equality
Sandwich
Oblong
Cave in Rock

Transportation

Major Interstate Highways

I-24, I-39, I-55, I-57, I-64, I-70, I-72, I-74, I-80, I-88, I-90, I-94
More than 130,000 miles (209,215 kilometers) of roads connect Illinois and the rest of the nation.

Railroads

Since 1856, when the Illinois Central Railroad was completed, railroads have played an important role in Illinois' leading export economy.

Major Airport

Chicago's O'Hare International Airport is one of the world's busiest airports.

Ports

Chicago and East St. Louis, two of Illinois' important ports, are among the busiest in the nation.

Timeline

1673 French explorers Jolliet and Marquette enter Illinois

1680 La Salle establishes Fort Créve Coeur near Peoria

1717 Illinois becomes part of French colony of Louisiana

1779 Du Sable establishes trading post near Chicago

1784 United States takes control of Illinois region

1794 Native Americans forced to give their land to the U.S.

1800 Illinois becomes part of the Indiana territory

1803 U.S. troops build Ft. Dearborn near Du Sable's post

1809 Illinois Territory is formed

1818 Illinois admitted to the Union

1832 Sauk and Fox Indians driven out of Illinois

1837 Springfield becomes the state capital

1860 Abraham Lincoln elected president

1865 Illinois first state to ratify the 13th Amendment

1871 Chicago fire destroys much of the city

1970 State constitution adopted

1973 Sears Tower completed

2001 Illinois enters 21st century!

Here come the humans!

Thousands of years ago, Paleo (ancient) people lived in Illinois. They may have originally come across a frozen bridge of land between Asia and today's Alaska. If so, they slowly traveled south and east until some settled in what would one day become the state of Illinois. By 900 C.E., a very organized culture had developed along the Mississippi River. Copper from as far away as Lake Superior and seashells from the Gulf of Mexico have been found in Illinois Indian mounds. By 1500 C.E. the Cahokia Mound site had been abandoned, but other Native American tribes continued to live throughout the Illinois area.

Native Americans Once Ruled!

The Illini Indians, who may have been related to the prehistoric mound builders, lived in the area at the time of the first European settlers. For 100 years, they lived in peace. Then, the Iroquois, who had traded with the English and Dutch, overpowered the Illini with with an effective new weapon—guns. The Illini were forced to move west, out of Illinois.

Word Definition

WAMPUM: beads, pierced and strung, used by Indians as money, or for ornaments or ceremonies.

Bonjour!

In 1673, Jacques Marquette and Louis Jolliet became the first Europeans to enter present day Illinois. They led five other men who travelled in canoes from Canada along the coast of Lake Michigan, through Wisconsin, and down the Mississippi to Illinois. These were the first of many Frenchmen who explored the area. The French already had established settlements in Canada, and wanted to extend their control southward into the heart of the continent.

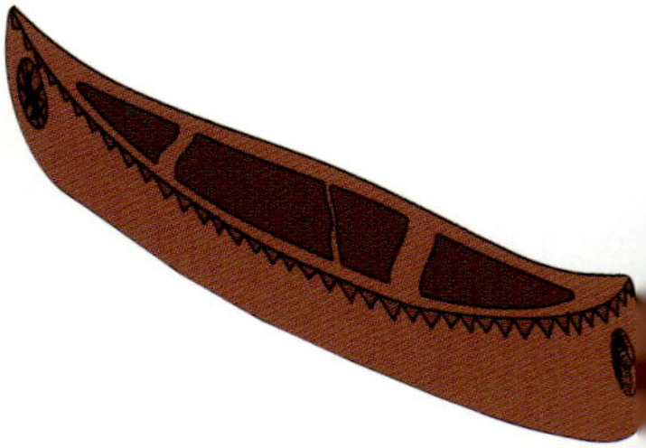

Home, Sweet, Home

Illinois was claimed early on by the Spanish, English, and the French. At the peak of French settlement, only about 2000-3000 colonists lived in the area.

By the time Illinois became a state, only the southern third of the state was settled. Many of the first Americans to settle in Illinois came from southern states. Some of them traveled in horse drawn wagons along the Cumberland Road which ended in Vandalia, Illinois.

The first job a settler had was to build a house. Most houses were one room with no windows. They were built of logs and a dirt floor.

Tractor Pull

Illinois has long been known for its contributions to agriculture. John Deere was a blacksmith who helped establish the area as an agricultural center by reshaping the plow and adapting it to the tough sod and prairie grasses. Cyrus McCormick was an Illinois resident who is credited with inventing a reaper for harvesting wheat. Caterpillar, based in Peoria, is the #1 producer of earth-moving equipment in the world. Soybeans, hogs, and corn are all important Illinois products today.

De Kalb county is known as the Barbed Wire Capital of the World. Invented by Joseph F. Glidden, barbed wire keeps animals from breaking through fences.

Fact Or Fiction?

- Outlaws of Cave-in-Rock were pirates who terrorized boaters on the Ohio River!
- Woodhenge at Cahokia Mounds preserves a mysterious site which might have been used in an ancient religious ceremony!
- Pictures of a monstrous bird were painted by Illini Indians near a cave on the Mississippi River, frightening explorers who wondered if the bird could actually be real!

Legends & Lore

Freedom!

Some settlers in the New World felt that British rulers ignored their ideas and concerns. In 1775, the colonies went to war with England. On July 4, 1776, the Declaration of Independence was signed. George Rogers Clark led a few hundred frontiersmen and pushed the British out of Kaskaskia. On July 4, 1778, the people celebrated the arrival of Clark by ringing the town bell. Since then the bell has been called the Liberty Bell of the West.

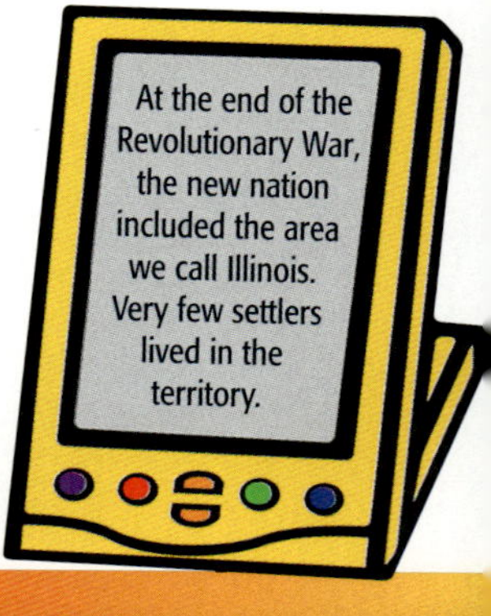

Of Human Bondage

Slavery existed in Illinois as far back as French colonial days. The Northwest Ordinance of 1787, issued by the United States, outlawed bringing new slaves into the territory, but did not free slaves already living in Illinois. The Illinois Constitution was changed in 1848 to abolish slavery throughout the state. The issue of slavery and states' rights led to the Civil War. In 1863, the Emancipation Proclamation freed slaves in areas still under Confederate control. In 1865, Illinois became the first state to ratify the 13th Amendment abolishing slavery in the United States.

Word Definition

ABOLITIONIST: person who believed slavery was wrong and should be abolished.

Brother

The Civil War was fought between the American states. The argument was over the right of the states to make their own decisions, including whether or not to own slaves. Some of the southern states began to secede (leave) the Union. They formed the Confederate States of America. Illinois remained loyal to the United States.

Word Definition

RECONSTRUCTION: the recovery and rebuilding period following the Civil War.

vs. Brother

Two important Illinoisans in the Civil War were Abraham Lincoln and Ulysses S. Grant. Lincoln was the President of the United States during the Civil War and credited for freeing the slaves. Grant became a Union General and led the Army of the Potomac. Confederate General Robert E. Lee surrendered to Grant at the end of the Civil War. The 7th Illinois Infantry was one of the first to carry repeating rifles, a big advantage over the single-shot muskets carried by other soldiers.

Get It In Writing!

Declaration of Independence, 1776

Northwest Ordinance, 1787

U.S. Constitution, 1787
The Constitution went into effect in 1789.

1st State Constitution, 1818

1848, New State Constitution; abolishes slavery

Dred Scott Supreme Court ruling, 1857

Present Illinois Constitution adopted in 1970

Welcome To America!

Illinoisans have come to the state from other states and many other countries on almost every continent! As time has gone by, Illinois' population has grown more diverse. This means that people of different races and from different cultures and ethnic backgrounds have moved to the state.

In the past, many immigrants came to Illinois from Great Britain, France, Germany, Hungary, and other European countries. Slaves migrated (involuntarily) from Africa. More recently, people have migrated to Illinois from Latin American, South American, and Asian countries. Nearly 75% of the U.S. Latino population lives in CA, TX, NY, FL, NJ, and Illinois, especially in the Chicago area. In the 1960s, following the Cuban Revolution, many Cubans immigrated to Chicago.

1871

The Chicago fire destroyed the city, killed 300, and left 90,000 residents homeless! It destroyed millions of dollars worth of property!

1903

A fire at the Irequois Theater in Chicago killed 571 people!

1915

The *Eastland*, an excursion boat, capsized in the Chicago River, killing 812 people!

1919

Race riots in Chicago killed 39 people and injured hundreds more!

1925

In a single tornado that ripped through Illinois, 603 people lost their lives! More than 1,000 Illinoisans have been killed by tornadoes since 1916!

Legal Stuff

1787

Following the American Revolution, the Northwest Ordinance laid the groundwork for settling new territories previously held by Britain.

1865

Illinois became the first state to ratify the 13th Amendment abolishing slavery.

1903

Illinois became the first state to limit child labor. In **1904,** child labor ended in the mines of Illinois!

1913

Women in Illinois were given the right to vote in presidential elections.

1919

The Illinois General Assembly ratified the 19th Amendment to the U.S. Constitution giving full voting rights to women. In **1920,** the 19th Amendment became law!

Women

1833

Jacksonville Female Seminary, the first Illinois institution of higher learning for women, was opened. The Ladies Education Society was also started in Jacksonville.

1912

President William Taft appointed Julia Lathrop to be the first head of the United States Children's Bureau which led the way in juvenile and maternal care nationwide.

1970

State constitution expanded Illinois' bill of rights protecting rights of women and people with disabilities.

1979

Jane Byrne became first woman elected Mayor of Chicago.

1992

Mary Ann G. McMorrow became the first female justice of the Illinois Supreme Court.

Word Definition

SUFFRAGE: the right or privilege of voting

Fight!, Fight!, Fight!

Wars that Illinoisans participated in:

- **French and Indian War**
- **Revolutionary War**
- **War of 1812**
- **Black Hawk War**
- **Mexican-American War**
- **Civil War**
- **Spanish-American War**
- **World War I**
- **World War II**
- **Korean War**
- **Vietnam War**
- **Persian Gulf War**

Land of Lincoln

Abraham Lincoln was the 16th President of the United States. Known for his famous speeches against slavery, Lincoln debated Stephen A. Douglas who believed states should decide for themselves whether or not to allow slavery. In 1860, Lincoln was elected President. His leadership held America together during its most difficult time–the Civil War years. In 1863, Lincoln issued the Emancipation Proclamation. In 1865, the 13th Amendment, which Lincoln planned and approved, outlawed slavery throughout the nation. He was assassinated by John Wilkes Booth at Ford's Theatre in Washington, D.C. in April 1865. Many historians think Abraham Lincoln was our greatest president!

Indian Tribes

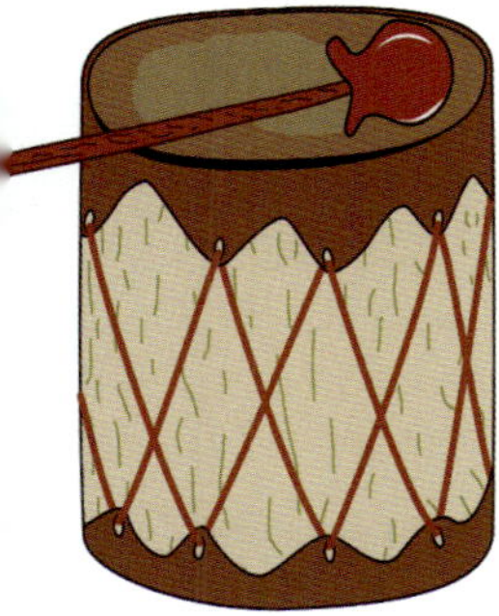

- Illini
  - Peoria
  - Kaskaskia
  - Tamaroa
  - Cahokia
  - Michigamea
- Miami, Shawnee, Kickapoo, Sauk, Fox, Ojibwa, Ottawa, Osage, Potawatomi, Delaware, Huron, Winnebago, Mascoutin, Assegun, Piankashaw, Tionontati

The Illini all spoke Algonquin, a group of languages shared by various tribes who lived all over the eastern half of North America.

In 1828, gold was discovered on Cherokee land in the Southeast. They tried to protect their land, but in 1838, the U.S. government forced the Cherokee Indians to leave their homes. Their march along the "Trail of Tears" to Oklahoma took them through southern Illinois. They were stranded for weeks by bad weather, during which many Cherokees died. The site in Jonesboro has been preserved as a state forest.

Here, There, Everywhere!

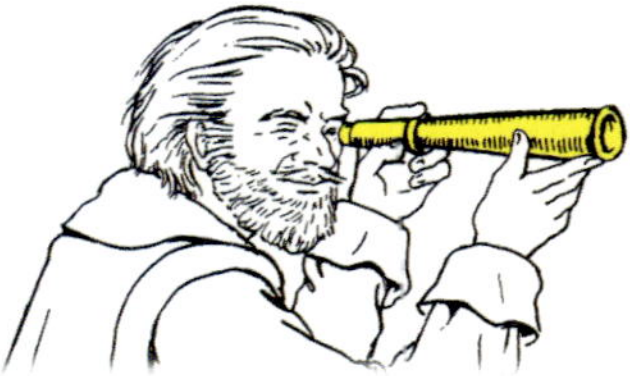

FATHER JACQUES MARQUETTE, a French priest, and LOUIS JOLLIET, a French soldier, traveled to Illinois from Canada.

JEAN BAPTISTE POINT DU SABLE was the French speaking Haitian pioneer who built a log cabin near the mouth of the Chicago River. He began trading with the Native Americans. His trading post prospered and became the center of a permanent Chicago settlement. Du Sable is regarded as the founder of Chicago.

RENÉ-ROBERT CAVELIER, SIEUR DE LA SALLE was the French explorer who built two forts on the Illinois River. Fort Creve Coeur was established near present-day Peoria and Fort Saint Louis was built atop Starved Rock overlooking the river.

Founding Fathers

These Illinoisans played especially important roles in the creation of the United States of America!

JOHN KINZIE was one of Illinois' earliest settlers who established a trading post in 1804 near Fort Dearborn on the site of present-day Chicago.

NATHANIEL POPE was the Illinois Territory Representative to the U.S. Congress who led the movement to make Illinois a state. He also helped draw the map of the new state and argued that the Illinois border should include a shoreline on Lake Michigan. DANIEL POPE COOK, the nephew of Nathaniel Pope, helped his uncle campaign to make Illinois a state.

Abolitionist ELIJAH P. LOVEJOY, minister turned newspaper editor, used his newspaper in Alton to share his views on the evils of slavery. His brother, OWEN LOVEJOY, shared Elijah's hatred of slavery and helped slaves escape on the Underground Railroad.

ELY PARKER, a Seneca Indian, knew Ulysses S. Grant from Galena. He became Grant's military aide during the Civil War and wrote the terms of surrender that officially ended the war.

Founding Mothers

MRS. NATHAN HEALD fought bravely during the Fort Dearborn Massacre alongside her husband, the fort's commanding officer.

MARY TODD LINCOLN was the wife of Abraham Lincoln.

FLORENCE KELLEY, a social worker and reformer, was appointed the state's first Chief of State Factory Inspection Department by President William Taft.

DR. MARY HARRIS THOMPSON, the nation's first female surgeon, founded the Chicago Hospital for Women and Children.

In 1832, during the Black Hawk War, a fort on the Apple River was attacked by more than 200 Indians. Settlers rushed to the fort where their defense was led by Elizabeth Armstrong because the men were away. Elizabeth and company successfully defended the fort! The town was later named in her honor.

Husband and wife, JOHN and MARY RICHARDSON, were anti-slavery and civil rights activists in Chicago in the 1800s. They fought against the discriminatory Black Laws which were repealed in 1865. They were also proponents of the the 13th, 14th, and 15th Amendments to the U.S. Constitution.

JOHN H. JOHNSON is the founder of Johnson Publishing Company which publishes *Ebony*, *Jet*, and *EM (Ebony Man)* and is the most successful African-American publishing company in the world. LINDA JOHNSON RICE is now president and one of the first women in the U.S. to run a major publishing company.

CAROL MOSELEY-BRAUN was elected to the Illinois State House of Representatives and later became the first African-American woman elected to the U.S. Senate.

RICHARD WRIGHT moved to Chicago when he was 19. His book *Native Son* was published in 1940 and made him the leading African-American author in the U.S.

DR. MAE JEMISON grew up in Chicago and became the first African-American woman in space aboard the space shuttle *Endeavor*.

OSCAR DEPRIEST was a Chicago city councilman who became the first African-American U.S. Congressman from Illinois.

DID SOMEONE SAY BOO!?

In 1878, Mary Lurancy Vennum, a 13-year-old girl from Milford, had been visited by ghosts and spirits for three years. She became possessed by the spirit of Mary Roff, the daughter of a family friend who'd been dead for 12 years. The families were so accepting of the fact that Mary was possessed by Mary's spirit that she moved in with the Roff family (pretty confusing isn't it?). She knew everything that the real Mary would have known although she was an infant when Mary died. This went on for several months, when at last, Mary Vennum awoke to find herself living in the wrong house. Mary Vennum went back home, and except for occasional visits from her old friend, Mary Roff, Mary Vennum became her old self!

DO YOU BELIEVE IN GHOSTS?

Sports Figures

P.K. WRIGLEY—Owner of the Chicago Cubs; started the first professional women's baseball league in the country–the All-Girls Professional Baseball League

ROBIN YOUNT—Milwaukee Brewers outfielder–American League's Most Valuable Player in 1982 and 1989

BETTY ROBINSON—Olympic track champion - first woman to win a track & field event

MICHAEL JORDAN—Chicago Bulls basketball great

GEORGE MIKAN—Basketball Hall of Famer

ANDREW "RUBE" FOSTER—African-American ballplayer; organized National Negro League

DICK BUTKUS—Football Hall of Famer

CASSIUS CLAY aka MUHAMMAD ALI—Heavyweight boxing champion

JACKIE JOYNER-KERSEE—Olympic track champion

BONNIE BLAIR—Olympic speed skating champion

SYBIL BAUER—Olympic swimming champion

GEORGE HANCOCK—created the game of softball in 1887

Entertainers

- JOHNNY WEISSMULLER—champion swimmer; movie star–*Tarzan*
- MARLEE MATLIN—actress; first deaf person to win an Academy Award for an acting role
- JACK BENNY—comedian
- FLORENZ ZIEGFELD—Broadway showman
- BOB NEWHART—comedian
- WALTER KOENIG—actor: "Pavel Chekov" on *Star Trek*
- JOSEPHINE BAKER—dancer and comedienne
- BOB FOSSE—dancer, choreographer, producer
- ANN-MARGRET—actress, singer, dancer
- HARRISON FORD—actor
- QUINCY JONES—composer, musician, conductor, arranger, trumpeter
- MILES DAVIS—jazz trumpeter
- OPRAH WINFREY—actress and entertainer
- ELIZABETH McGOVERN—actress
- BENNY GOODMAN—clarinetist, band leader
- ROBIN WILLIAMS—actor

RIDDLE: Which person on the list above is famous for saying, "Me, Tarzan! You, Jane!"?

ANSWER: Johnny Weissmuller

Authors

- **EDGAR LEE MASTERS**—poet
- **BETTY FRIEDAN**—feminist and author
- **RAY BRADBURY**—sci-fi writer
- **RAYMOND CHANDLER**—writer
- **VACHEL LINDSAY**—poet
- **JAMES T. FARRELL**—writer
- **ALISON LURIE**—writer, Pulitzer Prize
- **SAUL BELLOW**—writer, Nobel Prize
- **GWENDOLYN BROOKS**—Poet Laureate, Pulitzer Prize
- **EDGAR RICE BURROUGHS**—writer, newspaper correspondent, wrote *Tarzan of the Apes*
- **CARL SANDBURG**—poet, biographer, Pulitzer Prize
- **HARRIET MONROE**—editor; writer; creator of *Poetry: A Magazine of Verse*
- **ERNEST HEMINGWAY**—writer, journalist, Nobel Prize
- **EUGENE FIELD**—poet and journalist
- **MIKE ROYKO**—columnist, Pulitzer Prize
- **LORRAINE HANSBERRY**—playwright
- **SHEL SILVERSTEIN**—children's author
- **UPTON SINCLAIR**—writer and social reformer
- **SAM SHEPARD**—author, acto
- **JOHN DOS PASSOS**—novelis
- **JAMES SCHUYLER**—poet
- **LOUIS (STUDS) TERKEL**—social historian, Pulitzer Prize
- **JOHN JAKES**—writer

?????? Which famous poet gave Chicago its nickname: "Hog Butcher for the World?"

Answer: Carl Sandburg

Artists & More

WALT DISNEY—cartoonist; movie-maker; amusement-park creator

LOUIS HENRI SULLIVAN—architect, leader of Chicago School of Architecture

FRANK LLOYD WRIGHT—architect

DANIEL HUDSON BURNHAM—architect

CHIC YOUNG—cartoonist, creator of "Blondie"

CHESTER GOULD—cartoonist, creator of "Dick Tracy"

ALEXANDRA HAEGER ESTES—Haeger Potteries

CARRIE JACOBS BOND—painter and songwriter

LOREDO TAFT—sculptor

JOHN DAVID MOONEY—"light" artist

FLORENCE BEATRICE SMITH PRICE—first African-American woman to have a work, *Symphony in E Minor*, performed by a major orchestra–the Chicago Symphony Orchestra

HAROLD GRAY—cartoonist, creator of "Little Orphan Annie"

ELZIE CRISLER "E.C." SEGAR—creator of "Popeye"

HELEN HOKINSON—cartoonist whose work appeared in *The New Yorker* magazine

MALVINA HOFFMAN—sculptor

Very Important People

JOHN DEERE—farm equipment inventor/manufacturer; introduced first steel plow and first riding plow

GEORGE W. FERRIS—engineer; invented Ferris Wheel for World's Columbian Exposition in 1893

ELLA FLAG YOUNG—first woman in the U.S. to head a major metropolitan school system; Superintendent of Chicago schools

MARSHALL FIELD—merchant; established Marshall Field & Company in Chicago which became the world's largest retail store

WILLIAM WRIGLEY, JR.—manufacturer; founded William Wrigley, Jr. Company; maker of chewing gum

BLACK HAWK—Sauk Indian Leader

POTTER PALMER—merchant and real estate promoter

Very Important People

FRANK DRAKE—astronomer; conducted the first organized search for extraterrestrial life

GROTE REBER—invented the first radio telescope—in his backyard!

PHILIP ARMOUR—industrialist; leading innovator in meat packing industry; formed Armour & Company

BLACK PARTRIDGE—Potawatomi chief

JOSEPH SMITH—founder and first president of the Mormon Church; founded Mormon community of Nauvoo

Confectioners **F.W. RUECKHEIM**–Crackerjack; **OTTO SCHNERING**–Baby Ruth; **FRANK BRACH**–candy corn, chocolate covered peanuts, Starlight Mints

More VIPs

BRIGHAM YOUNG—Mormon missionary

CLARENCE DARROW—defense attorney

ENRICO FERMI—physicist, Nobel Prize

CYRUS McCORMICK—inventor and industrialist, invented reaping machine

Cousins **ROBERT R. McCORMICK** and **JOSEPH MEDILL PATTERSON**—editors and publishers of the *Chicago Tribune*

MONTGOMERY WARD—founded Montgomery Ward & Company, world's first mail-order business

FRANCES E. WILLARD—president of the Women's Christian Temperance Union which supported women's suffrage and Prohibition

WARREN SEARS/ALVAH C. ROEBUCK—founders and **JULIUS ROSENWALD**—president and chairman of the board of Sears, Roebuck & Co.

JAMES BUTLER (WILD BILL) HICKOK—scout, frontiersman, U.S. Marshal

GEORGE ROGERS CLARK—led Kentucky frontiersmen on an important campaign to push the British out of Illinois during the Revolutionary War

ALLAN PINKERTON—investigator, opened first detective agency in U.S.; guarded Abraham Lincoln on inaugural journey from Springfield to the U.S. capitol, Washington, D.C.

WYATT EARP—U.S. Marshal, famous for shootout at the O.K. Coral in Tombstone, Arizona

FLORENCE FIFER BOHRER—first woman elected to the Illinois senate

GOOD GALS/GUYS

- SAINT FRANCES XAVIER CABRINI, a Roman Catholic nun, was the first American citizen to be canonized. She founded Chicago's Columbus Hospital.
- JANE ADDAMS, a social worker and reformer, was the first American woman to be awarded the Nobel Peace Prize. She fought for civil liberties and better living conditions, and founded the Hull House in Chicago with ELLEN GATES STARR.
- WILLIAM D. BOYCE, a Chicago publisher, founded the Boy Scouts of America.
- DANIEL HALE WILLIAMS, an Illinois surgeon, helped improve opportunities for African-Americans in medicine. He founded Provident Hospital in Chicago.
- Mary Ann Bickerdyke, known as MOTHER BICKERDYKE, was a nurse and social reformer who worked to clean up and organize dirty Civil War hospitals.

VERY BAD GUY: AL CAPONE, a hit-man and gangster, was involved in many illegal activities in Chicago during the 1920s. He was responsible for the 1929 St. Valentine's Day Massacre in which rival gang members were killed. He was finally arrested and sent to prison for tax evasion in 1931.

Political Leaders

- HILLARY RODHAM CLINTON—First Lady from 1992 to 2000
- SHADRACH BOND—1st governor of Illinois
- JOHN PETER ALTGELD—lawyer, governor
- JANE BYRNE—Chicago's first female mayor
- RONALD REAGAN—40th U.S. President
- ULYSSES S. GRANT—18th U.S. President
- U.S. Vice President ADLAI E. STEVENSON and son, ADLAI E. STEVENSON II, governor and U.S. ambassador to the United Nations
- HAROLD WASHINGTON—first black mayor of Chicago
- EVERETT DIRKSEN—U.S. Senator
- WILLIAM JENNINGS BRYAN—lawyer, politician, orator
- STEPHEN A. DOUGLAS—U.S. Senator, U.S. Congressman, ran unsuccessful race for president against Abraham Lincoln
- RICHARD J. DALEY and son, RICHARD M. DALEY—mayors of Chicago
- JAMES R. THOMPSON—four term governor
- LUIS GUTIERREZ—first Hispanic elected to the U.S. Congress from Illinois
- JOHN PAUL STEVENS—U.S. Supreme Court Justice

Keeping the Faith

The Church of the Assumption - in Chicago was founded by Mother Frances Xavier Cabrini.

Baha'i Temple - in Wilmette is the North American headquarters of the Baha'i religion.

Nauvoo - is the restored site of a temple, homes, and several buildings that once belonged to a Mormon community lead by Joseph Smith and Brigham Young.

SCHOOLS

Some of Illinois' colleges and universities:

- University of Illinois - Champaign-Urbana
- University of Illinois - Chicago
- University of Chicago
- Northwestern University
- Loyola University
- Art Institute of Chicago
- Northern Illinois
- Southern Illinois
- Western Illinois
- Eastern Illinois
- Northeastern Illinois
- Illinois State
- Lake Forest College
- Illinois Institute of Technology

Historic Sites and Parks

Historic Sites

★ Bishop Hill
★ Fort de Chartres
★ John Deere Historic Site
★ Lovejoy Monument
★ Cahokia Mounds
★ Dickson Mounds

Parks

★ Shawnee National Forest—in southern Illinois covers about 270,000 acres (109,265 hectares)

★ Pére Marquette State Park—located where the Mississippi and Illinois rivers meet

★ Buffalo Rock State Park—a restored coal mine with huge earthen sculptures is a refuge for wildlife

★ Fox Ridge State Park — near Charleston contains the Trail of Trees

★ Moraine Hills State Park — near McHenry, has ice-fishing, cross-country skiing and snowmobiling!

Illinois has five state forests, seventy-three state parks, and two state marinas!

Early Residency

★ **Lincoln Log Cabin** - in Lerna was the last home of Abraham Lincoln's parents.

★ **Lincoln's Home** - in Springfield, was the only home that Abraham Lincoln ever owned. He later became the sixteenth U.S. President.

★ **Carl Sandburg Birthplace** - in Galesburg, is a three-room cottage purchased by the author's parents in 1873.

★ **Ulysses S. Grant Home** - in Galena, is the house that Grant and his family lived in after he returned from the Civil War in 1865. Grant later became the eighteenth U.S. President.

★ **New Salem Village** - in Petersburg, is a reproduction of the village where the Lincoln family lived from 1831-1837.

★ **Reagan Home** - in Dixon, is the childhood home of Ronald Reagan. He later became the fortieth U.S. President

A few of Illinois' famous Battles

THE FRENCH AND INDIAN WAR - By the 1700s the French had settled in villages along the Mississippi River in southern Illinois. They planned to start a new French empire. Then in 1756 war broke out between France and Britain. By 1763 the British had defeated the French and won control of France's possessions, including Illinois.

THE WAR OF 1812 - The U.S. and Britain were at war again. The Native Americans sided with the British and attacked American forts. Fort Dearborn in Illinois is the site of a famous attack. In 1814 both countries signed the Treaty of Ghent and ended the war.

THE BLACK HAWK WAR - In 1832 the Sauk and Fox Indians tried to stop the new white settlers from taking over their land. The U.S. Army and the Illinois militia fought back. The Indians were defeated.

Libraries

Check-out the following special state libraries! (Do you have a library card? Have you worn it out yet?!)

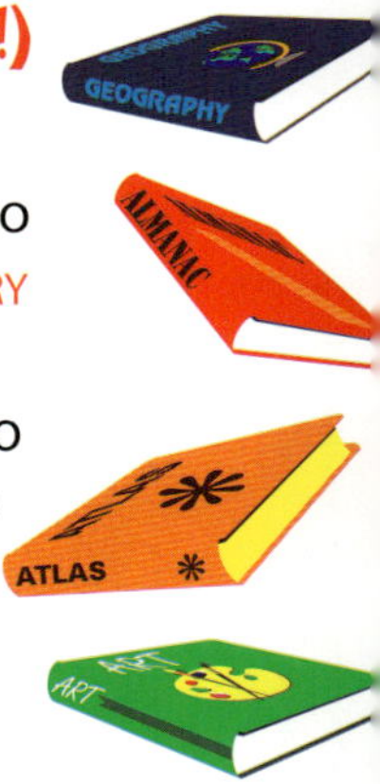

- CHICAGO PUBLIC LIBRARY — Chicago
- THE ILLINOIS STATE HISTORICAL LIBRARY — Springfield
- CRERAR SCIENCE LIBRARY — Chicago
- THE NEWBERRY LIBRARY — Chicago
- THE UNIVERSITY OF ILLINOIS LIBRARY — Champaign-Urbana

Zoos & Attractions

Lincoln Park Zoo — Chicago
The Adler Planetarium — Chicago
John G. Shedd Aquarium — Chicago
Chicago Botanical Garden — Glencoe
Glen Oak Zoo — Peoria
Cernan Earth and Space Center — River Grove
Starhill Forest Arboretum — Petersburg
Henson Robinson Zoo — Springfield
Washington Park Botanical Garden — Springfield
Chicago Zoological Park — Brookfield
Morton Arboretum — Lisle
Great America Amusement Park— Gurnee
Wildlife Prairie Park — Peoria
Super Man Statue and Celebration — Metropolis
Garfield Park Conservatory — River Grove

Museums

- Krannert Art Museum — Champaign
- Art Institute of Chicago — Chicago
- Chicago Children's Museum — Chicago
- Hauberg Indian Museum — Rock Island
- Illinois State Museum — Springfield
- Oriental Institute Museum — Chicago
- Field Museum of Natural History — Chicago
- Museum of Contemporary Art — Chicago
- Museum of the Chicago Academy of Sciences — Chicago
- DuSable Museum of African-American History — Chicago
- Lakeview Museum for Arts and Sciences — Peoria
- Burpee Museum of Natural History — Rockford
- Terra Museum of American Art — Evanston

Lest We Forget

LINCOLN'S TOMB - in Springfield, is the burial site of Abraham Lincoln, his wife Mary Todd Lincoln, and three of their sons

LOVEJOY MONUMENT - in Alton, honors the good deeds of abolitionist Elijah Lovejoy

HULL HOUSE - in Chicago, is the original site of the Hull House founded by Jane Addams in 1889

Famous Places

ROBIE HOUSE - built by Frank Lloyd Wright in 1909, is an example of his "prairie style" architecture

WRIGLEY FIELD - home to the National League Chicago Cubs

COMISKY PARK - home to the American League Chicago White Sox

How will it play in Peoria?

THE CHICAGO SYMPHONY ORCHESTRA — considered to be best in the world

LYRIC OPERA — Chicago's own major opera company

HUBBARD STREET DANCE COMPANY— Chicago

CHICAGO CITY BALLET

A RAISIN IN THE SUN — a story about growing up in Chicago

SHUBERT THEATER — Chicago

Lakefronts

The Northeastern corner of Illinois lies on Lake Michigan, one of the five Great Lakes.

Lighthouses

The Chicago Harbor lighthouse was so impressive that the light was on exhibit at the Columbian Exhibition in Chicago in 1893.

ROADS

THE NATIONAL ROAD — the first federal highway, started in Virginia and ended in Vandalia, Illinois!

BRIDGES AND CANALS

THE ILLINOIS AND MICHIGAN CANAL — the 96 mile (154 km) canal connected Lake Michigan with the Illinois River

THE ILLINOIS AND MISSISSIPPI CANAL — connected the Illinois and Mississippi Rivers

SANITARY AND SHIP CANAL — built in 1900; to direct sewage away from the city, engineers reversed the flow of the Chicago River!

WILLIAM F. DEAN BRIDGE — the only suspension bridge in the state is now a restored walkway over the Kaskaskia River

RED COVERED BRIDGE — built in 1863 near Princeton, one of five original covered bridges still standing in Illinois

Prairies and Wetlands

PRAIRIES

Illinois is known as the Prairie State. Early settlers wrote home about the vast fields of grass and wildflowers. The prairie was beautiful, but it was dense with tough roots that made farming difficult.

Today, several prairies are being preserved by the Illinois Nature Conservatory. **The Nashua Grasslands**, near Dixon, is a 700 acre (280 hectare) site of prairie grass, plants, flowers, and animals. The Illinois Dunes State Park is one of the state's largest preserved prairies.

WETLANDS

Cache River Wetlands - in southern Illinois, are now being preserved by the Nature Conservatory. Forty percent of Illinois' endangered species call the wetlands home.

The American Bottom - a floodplain between the Mississippi River and the bluffs near Kaskaskia. Early settlers found the fertile soil great for farming.

The oldest living things east of the Mississippi River are the prehistoric cypress trees in the Cache River Wetlands. Some of the trees are nearly one thousand years old!

Animals of Illinois

Illinois' animals include:

White-tailed Deer
Albino Squirrel
Opossum
Raccoon
Wood Rat
Prairie Dog
Fox
Skunk
Squirrel
Rabbit
Prairie Chicken
Beaver
Mink

Take A Walk On the Wild Side

The Mark Twain National Wildlife Refuge, covers land in three states including 16, 579 acres (6,331 hectares) in Illinois. Wood Ducks nest in the refuge.

The Upper Mississippi River National Wildlife Refuge, covers 3,300 acres (1,320 hectares) of land in Illinois. The refuge has become an important area for the Bald Eagle.

Crab Orchard National Wildlife Refuge, covers 43,600 acres (17,440 hectares) next to a maximum security prison! Nearly 2 million birds visit each year.

Birds

You may spy these birds!

Red-Winged Blackbirds

Ringneck Pheasants

Purple Martins

Bobwhite Quails

Canadian Geese

Wood Duck

American Crows

Bald Eagles

Hummingbirds

Bluejays

Chickadees

Wild Turkeys

Sparrows

Snow Geese

Blue Geese

Waterfowl

A hummingbird's wings beat 75 times a second– so fast that you only see a blur! They make short, squeaky sounds, but do not sing.

Don't let these Illinois bugs bug you!

Beetle
Cicada
Cricket
Dragonfly
Firefly
Honeybee
Katydid
Mayfly
Mosquito
Moth
Termite
Walking Stick
Weevil
Yellow Jacket

Bumblebee

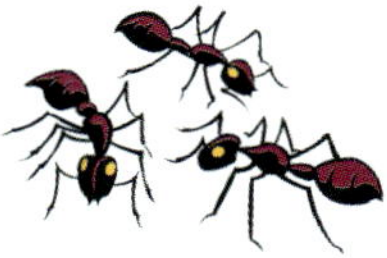
Ants

Butterfly

Praying Mantis

Ladybug

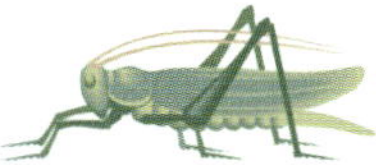
Grasshopper

Whirligig Beetles have two pairs of eyes – one pair looks above the water, the other looks under it!

You can spot these fish in Illinois' lakes and rivers;

Bass
Bluegill
Buffalo Fish
Carp
Catfish
Crappie
Lake Trout
Northern Pike
Perch
Salmon
Sauger
Smelt
Walleye
White Bass

Lake Michigan

Lake Michigan connects Illinois to major shipping ports throughout the world. Goods such as iron ore, steel, grain, coal, and manufactured goods are shipped into Chicago. Some of the goods stay in Illinois, but the rest are sent down the Mississippi River to people all over the country.

Lake Michigan has seen many shipwrecks in her day. In 1913, "The Christmas Tree Ship" was carrying evergreen trees to be sold at the Clark Street Dock in Chicago. A violent storm hit and the boat was lost in the waves!

Lake Michigan is the only one of the five Great Lakes that is entirely within the boundaries of the United States.

Yabba-Dabba-Doo!

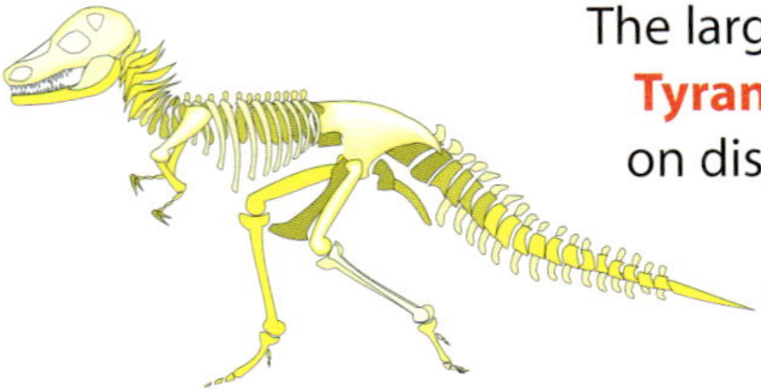

The largest skeleton of a **Tyrannosaurus Rex** is on display at Chicago's Field Museum. Her name is Sue!

Fossil Ridge is an area near Briarwood where numerous fossils have been found. Strip mining uncovered the ground, and nearly 700 species of animals and plants have been found.

Starved Rock is a magnificent outcropping of rock that overlooks the Illinois River. La Salle established a fort atop the rock in 1681. Today a staircase takes visitors to the top for a spectacular view.

Tower Rock is a 60-foot (18 meters) high rock on the Mississippi River. The rock is protected by the federal government, making it the smallest national park in America.

Cave-in-Rock, a cavern on the Ohio River, is 200 feet (60 meters) deep, with an opening 55 feet (16.6 meters) wide and 20 feet (6 meters) high! The cave once served as a hideout for bandits and river pirates!

TREEMENDOUS!

These trees tower over Illinois:

Oak
White Oak
Hickory
Walnut
Hard Maple
Sycamore
Elm
Tamarack
Bald Cypress
Tupelo Gum
Cottonwood

Wildflowers

Wild Geranium
Native Violet
Snow Trillium
Bluebell
Goldenrod
Sunflower

Cream of the Crops

Agricultural products from Illinois.

Chickens

Corn

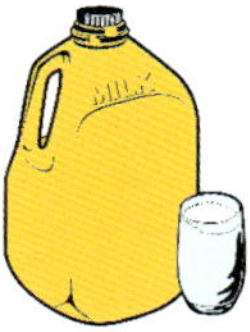

Milk

Hogs

Yams

Beef Cattle

Peaches

Apples

Wheat

Soybeans

Hay

First/Big/Small/Etc.

The CORNDOG was invented in Springfield.

MONKS MOUND at Cahokia Mounds State Historic Site is the largest in the U.S. It is 100 feet (30 meters) high and its base covers 16 acres (6.46 hectares).

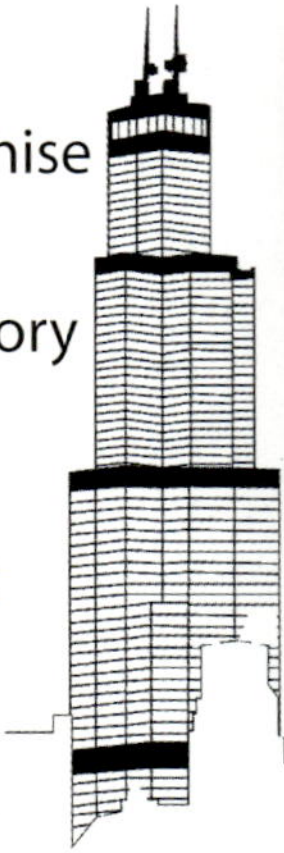

The first MCDONALDS fast-food franchise opened in Des Plaines in 1955.

The FIRST SKYSCRAPER was a ten story building built in Chicago in 1883.

The SEARS TOWER in Chicago is 110 stories high making it the tallest building in the United States.

The FIRST AMERICAN LEAGUE BASEBALL GAME was played in Chicago in 1901!

Illinois has more NUCLEAR POWER plants and gets more electricity from nuclear power than any other state.

The first FERRIS WHEEL was invented for the 1893 World's Columbian Exhibition in Chicago. It was 250 feet (76 meters) tall and each of its 36 cars could hold over 40 people!

Festivals

Central Illinois Jazz Festival - held every January in Decatur

St. Patricks Day Parade - in Chicago is one of the largest in the country!

Steam Boat Days And Race - held in June in Peoria

Cows on Parade - summer 1999, cows decorated by local artists were on display throughout Chicago. The cows were sold at auction and the money donated to charity.

Grape Festival - held Labor Day weekend in Nauvoo

Apple Festival - held every September in Long Grove

Pumpkin Festival - held in Sycamore in October, just in time for Halloween!

Lake Shelbyville Festival of Lights - a fabulous display of holiday lights held from November to January

Holidays

Calendar

Martin Luther King, Jr. Day, *3rd Monday in January*

Presidents' Day, *3rd Monday in February*

Pulaski Day, *the first Monday in March*

Memorial Day, *last Monday in May*

Independence Day, *July 4*

Columbus Day, *2nd Monday in October*

Veterans Day, *November 11*

Thanksgiving, *the last Thursday of November*

Christmas, *December 25*

Notes: ____________________

Memorial day was started by John Logan, a Civil War hero from Illinois!

Famous Food

Illinois is famous for the following delicious foods!

Corndog
Kolaches
Scrapple
Green Tomato Pickles
Horseshoe Sandwich
Deep Dish Pizza
Apple Pancakes
Sweet Corn
Wiener Schnitzel
Barbecue Ribs
Baked Yams
Blood Sausage
Porterhouse Steak
Corncob Jelly
Liver Dumplings

Illinois Works!

Agriculture
Corn
Soybeans
Hogs
Beef Cattle

Manufacturing
Food products
Machinery
Chemicals
Printed materials

Mining
Coal
Fluorspar
Petroleum
Tripoli

Business
John Deere
Marshall Fields
Sears Roebuck
Keebler
Zenith Radios
Montgomery Ward
Kraft Foods
Sara Lee
Wrigley's
Walgreens
Caterpillar